WITHDRAWN
From Toronto Public Library

DANNY IN A NEWFANGLED WORLD

Dannyinanewfangledworld.com

TO JOHN-DANIEL, PATRICK, AND COLE

All rights reserved. No portion of this book
may be reproduced, stored in a retrieval system,
or transmitted in any form or by any means,
mechanical, electronic, photocopying, recording,
or otherwise, without written permission, from the author.

ISBN 978-0-9866377-0-4

Copyright text & illustrations © Danielle Leonard
Book Illustrations by Celia Krampien
Book Design by Dwayne Harmer and Ryan Scheife, Mayfly Design

Published by Porridge Media
Oakville CANADA

Printed in Canada

The Problem with Blah Land

Danny Lenesky loved to play video games. They were as important to him as pizza was to parties, cannon balls to pools, and nose-picking to his little brother. In fact, there were no worse words in the whole world than "Danny, turn off the computer!"

Danny called it the *Mom Bomb*. She dropped it regularly and he was never prepared. That's why he could never surrender without a fight.

"*Aaaaw*, I'm not finished my game, Mom!" he would bellow.

"Just turn it off."

"But, Mo-o-o-om!"

"Off, young man."

They would toss words back and forth like a ping pong ball until Danny finally followed her orders. His parents just didn't get it. Didn't they see that there was nothing more important to Danny than knowing how to slide faster, smash harder, bounce higher, and think quicker than ever before in each game he played? In fact, there was no kid that he knew (at least in his grade) who came close to his video gaming talent.

His friends were in awe of him. His enemies were jealous of him. The only other kid in class that came close to such fame was Trey who recited the alphabet to the tune of his flatulence.

It was hilarious, Danny agreed. But even a melody of farts didn't interest him if the computer was on. He had only one thing on his mind. Winning every game he played. The downside was that he'd become so good that he'd mastered all of the games he knew. He would love to find new games, but there was one person blocking his way. Mom Lenesky.

"Stay in the safety zone," she reminded Danny whenever he turned on the computer (which happened to be quite frequently.) The safety zone was a bunch of web sites that she called danger-free. He'd always been content to play on those sites when he was younger, but he was ten years old now! And he'd had enough of this Blah Land. It was time to try something new. If only she'd let him.

Then one day, as he was blasting three-headed aliens on Mars (for the thousandth time), two shocking words slipped past his lips.

"I'm bored."

He covered his mouth. Had he actually said that? Danny couldn't believe it. How had it come to this? Boredom was supposed to happen at other times, like during spelling tests or while watching Teletubbies with his little brother. But playing video games? Never! How had his favourite thing in the whole world suddenly become as unappealing as a box of raisins at Halloween? He had to take action.

"Can I please go to other sites?" he begged his mother as she whisked past the room.

"Nope. But you can pick up the dirty socks in your room," she offered.

Danny pretended he didn't hear and fell silent while she walked upstairs. He propped his elbows up on the desk to stare at the computer screen. What now?

"Well, I guess I could just turn the computer off," he said.

Then he shook his head. How could he even consider such an idea? And then what would he do? Polish his LEGO? Count the books on his shelf? Sit on his basketball and stare at the road? No. It was no use. There just wasn't anything interesting to do. It was video games, or nothing. That's just the way it was.

He stared at the screen. The opening scene for the game *Road Rider* splashed across it. He moved the mouse over the *Play* button then stopped. He was sick of this game too. Maybe he should just shut the computer off.

"Don't do it," croaked a voice.

"Huh?" Danny looked around. "Who said that? Mom? Was that you?"

She didn't answer. She was probably too busy making a list of chores for him to do. He gave his head a shake. Hearing voices? Boy, he was really losing it now. As much as Danny hated to admit it, he'd had enough of the computer. It was time to turn it off and find something else to do — whatever that would be. Just as he was about to click on *Shut Down*, something caught his eye. In the bottom right corner of the computer screen a small blue button flashed.

A Little Button into a Big World

The button blinked. Danny leaned in very close and read its small print.

DO YOU DARE?

"Do I dare... what?" he asked. He clicked on it. A new button appeared with words as tiny as fruit flies. Danny ran to his parents' bedroom and retrieved his dad's magnifying glass. Holding it a few inches from the letters, he read:

PRESS IF YOU
WANT TO COME IN

Go inside a computer? Awesome! Of course he would. Wouldn't any kid? Duh, yeah!

He clicked the button. The screen turned black and enormous red letters flew like wild bats at him:

Danny's butt ejected out of his seat and he rushed head first into the computer screen then flew through a hallway that twisted like a serpent. Red and yellow lights flickered while the sounds of special effects exploded in his ears ...until he landed SMACK on a motorcycle.

The coloured lights must have blinded him, because all he saw was a silvery haze. He panicked.

"I'm blind! I'm blind!" he screamed.

He shut his stinging eyes and rubbed them with his knuckles. When he opened them again, the haze had disappeared and Danny discovered he was in the middle of an arena. He looked around. Cheers rang out from the stands where faceless fans glowing like light bulbs bounced up and down in their seats.

A black paved driveway led out of the arena and into a forest. Way in the distance was a massive grey wall that stretched so far up into the sky that if there had been a moon up there, the wall would certainly have reached it. Danny trembled with excitement just thinking about exploring all of this. He clasped his hands together. Clank! His hands were shiny and hard as glass. In fact, his entire body was. It was like he was covered in armour.

"Wicked!" he yelled, clicking his fingers against his cheeks. Clank-clank-clank.

A rumbling sound came from behind him. Danny turned to see a biker drive up to his side.

"Say your prayers, dude!" the biker said with a scowl.

His helmet read *Phantom* and he looked like one, too. He was ghostly white and dressed in a purple and pink jumpsuit. A shot sounded and Phantom took off. The race was on!

Danny pushed his motorcycle forward with his feet and cranked up the engine with a twist of his handlebars. He bent his head low and whizzed up behind Phantom where the trail made a sudden turn. Danny skidded off the track but straightened his bike just as he was about to crash into a tree. Phew... That was a close one! Phantom was still ahead, disappearing down a mountainside.

As Danny edged toward the top of the rocky mountain, his bike sputtered and slowed... Put-put-put-put. His gas meter read empty.

"Aw, come on!" he cried, "I need to fill up!"

Just then, he noticed a glassy red globe spinning in the sky. Danny putted toward it and pressed the 'jump' button on his dash. His bike sprang into the air and smashed the globe. Red jelly bits splattered all over him. When he landed, the gas meter was full and his bike lurched ahead so fast that his legs flew off the bike and wagged behind him like a dog's tail.

The path down the mountainside was littered with fallen trees, flat tires, jagged rocks, and rusted nails.

He zigged and zagged the track like a pro once he got the hang of it. He'd played this game many times before at home and remembered it well. He could probably even do it with his eyes closed, but thought it best not to try.

He caught up to Phantom quickly. They were neck and neck as they climbed the last ramp that rose like a tower into the sky. Danny inched ahead at the top then sprung off the edge and sailed across the air. As he approached the ground, he tilted his front tire up then landed on the pavement to pass the finish line first. Swirling ribbons danced all around him as Danny raised his arms in victory. He got off the bike and ran toward a sign that read EXIT with an arrow pointing at a door. He couldn't wait to see what came next. He pushed the door open and blazed through.

A Friend that's Blue

Rides and carnival games spread out in front of him. They reminded Danny of his favourite park, Super-Land, except that there were even more rides. And no line ups! There wasn't another kid in sight. They were all stuck at home looking through a screen. Suckerrrrs!

Now he had to decide what to do first. That was not easy. He recognized some games immediately. There was *PizzaGooGuy* over there, *Spazzit* just ahead, and *LolliPoppers* through the archway right in front of him. He rubbed his empty stomach. His mother always warned him to not eat too much sugar. "It'll fill you up and ruin your appetite," she would warn him. The *LolliPoppers* game provided an excellent opportunity to put her words to the test. How much sugar could he really eat anyway?

Danny ran through the opening to *Lollipoppers* and into a red tent big enough for two hundred kids (one hundred and seventy-six if they were the chunky lollipop-eating sort.) Lucky for Danny the tent was filled, instead, with gazillions of glistening lollipops that drifted like snowflakes. To catch them, he had to step off the floor and onto a web of tight ropes that stretched above a pit filled with cotton candy. As much as Danny loved pink floss, he had no desire to fall a few hundred feet just for a few mouthfuls.

"Step right up," announced a crackling voice. "Grab a lolli, get a point. Take a spill, you've had your fill."

Easing one foot and then the other onto a tight rope, Danny inched across the web. It wasn't so hard, after all, with so many criss-crossing ropes. Before long, he was reaching in every direction to grab as many lollipops as he could. Each catch exploded like a mini firework in his hand, then disappeared. Ching-ching-ching went the points. Above his head, his increasing score floated like a balloon. 180...190...200! Suddenly the cotton candy rose like a pot of boiling water toward Danny and tossed him into the air. The crackling voice announced, "Level one is done, level two for you!"

When Danny landed, he was on a kid-sized race track. At the start of the track was a gleaming red tricycle, much like the one he'd ridden when he was younger. What could be easier than riding a little kiddie bike? Piece of cake.

He lifted one leg over the tricycle and plopped his butt onto the small white seat. With his knees jutting out past the handlebars, he set his feet on the pedals and slowly wheeled forward.

Small candies pelted him like hail as he wobbled through the maze. The trike teetered to the side and almost fell over when he lifted an arm to grab a candy missile. He lifted his other arm and it teetered to the other side. No wonder he got rid of his trike when he was four, he realized, the dumb thing was useless for a big kid like him. Danny opened his mouth wide as he held fast to the handlebars, turning his head one way, then the other, to catch the sweets in his mouth. Much to his disappointment, each candy dissolved tastelessly the instant it touched his tongue.

Without warning, the tricycle bucked like a wild horse and threw Danny off. Rather than landing on the ground, he fell through the air as the race track disappeared like clouds on a sunny day.

"Level two is done, try level three for fun!" the announcer boomed.

Dozens of swinging trapezes dropped from the top of the tent. Danny grasped one. Not far ahead, he could see the grand prize. A huge green lollipop big enough to shoot hoops with. Danny couldn't wait. Dangling from his trapeze, he swung his body through the air. Suckers swarmed like bees around him, poking him in the face, tickling him in the arm pits, and tugging his body from the trapeze. He giggled so hard his stomach hurt and he almost lost his grip. To gain control he concentrated on things he hated (homework, baths, soggy cereal) and battled the candies with swats and kung fu kicks. From one trapeze to the next he jumped until the lollipop was within reach. Swinging toward it, he dove with his hands outstretched.

"Got it!" he yelled, his hands gripping the white stick attached to it.

"Congratulations," spoke the announcer. "You're a winner!" The lollipop flew Danny, like it was a witch's broom, to the tent's exit and landed outside the game.

He dismounted and, lifting the sweet treat to his mouth, closed his eyes, stuck out his tongue, and licked it. Huh? It tasted like nothing. It was as if he'd licked a huge marble. He tried again. Maybe the sweet part was in the center, like tootsie pops. He licked again and again and again. No taste. Zero. Zippo.

"Hey! What kind of place is this?" he said angrily. He'd been ripped off.

He dropped the candy and wandered away. Oh well, at least he'd had fun, he comforted himself. He eyed the pizza game as his stomach rumbled, but shook his head. He wouldn't be fooled again. He wasn't in the real world anymore. Things were different here.

He looked past all the games and noticed the huge wall that he'd seen earlier. It stood like a guard in the distance. What was it? And what was on the other side? It scared him a little, but thrilled him too. Whatever it was, he didn't need to worry about it now. There were too many games to play!

He jumped from one ride to the next. Some were like roller coasters, others were shooting games, and a few tested his math and spelling skills. He only did those ones when he needed to catch his breath. It's not like he missed school or anything.

He was having so much fun that he was surprised

when he looked up and saw that the he was right next to the wall. He'd soon have to turn around and find his way home. Just then he heard a tap-tap-tapping behind him. He swung around to see a small blue boy skipping along on one foot — the only one he had.

"Hi," the little guy called out.

"Hey," replied Danny.

The boy was coloured blue, right from his hair to the buttons on his top. He looked as though he was plucked right from a blueberry bush. He was skinny as a monkey and short too, his eyes level with the waist band on Danny's pants. Not only was he missing one foot, the leg normally attached to it was gone too. He was missing an arm, one ear, and the very tip of his nose which appeared to have been nipped off by an angry Chihuahua.

"I'm Jingo!" the blue boy announced, holding out his hand to Danny.

"Hi." Danny shook it. "I'm Danny. Uh, what happened to you?"

"Oh, you mean my missing parts?"

"Yeah, and you're blue!"

Jingo laughed, "I've always been blue. I'm from the video game Jingo Jango. You heard of it?"

Danny shook his head.

"It was destroyed by a virus. The game broke apart, and everyone got very sick. We started losing our body parts. My friend Jango eventually lost all his parts and disappeared. I survived. Somehow. Now I just wander alone."

"You don't have a home or a family?" Danny asked.

"It's just me," he shrugged.

"Well, we can be friends while I'm visiting," Danny said, feeling a little sorry for him.

Jingo's face brightened, "I'd like that very much, thank you. Are you having fun?"

"Oh yeah! Do you know if I'm the only kid from, you know, the real world?"

"No. There are lots of you who come and go. Anyone who stares at their computer screen long enough will eventually get sucked in. If they want to, that is. But not everyone sees the button. I'm so glad you did."

"And the voice. Was it you who talked to me? Did you say 'don't do it'?"

Jingo looked confused. "No. I didn't say anything."

"I'm sure I heard a voice," Danny said.

Jingo looked around nervously. "I don't know what that was."

He grabbed Danny's hand.

"Would you like to play with me now?" Jingo asked, leading him away from the wall.

"Wait a second," Danny flicked his head toward the grey wall. "What is that?"

He ran to it and pressed his hand against it. It was cold and dry. Tilting his head back, he stared as high as he could, yet he still could not see the top of the wall. Danny felt like an ant beside it.

Jingo shuddered, "You don't want to go past it."

"Actually, I do," Danny said. "I'm ready for some serious gaming! No more Blah Land."

"Walls are built for a reason. The bigger the wall, the more need for protection from what's on the other side."

"What is on the other side?" Danny asked, lifting an eyebrow.

Jingo set his one hand on his hip. "Some things are better left alone. This side you're safe. That side, you're not."

"Oh you sound like my parents!" said Danny. "I want to go."

"Once you pass the wall, you can never come back the way you came."

"Why not? I can just turn around."

"The paths change. You'll lose your way."

"Hmmm. Well, we can argue about it until I'm blue in the face too, but it doesn't matter. I can't see any way of getting past this wall." He shrugged and walked away from it.

Suddenly he heard a soft cre-e-eak.

"Where are you going?" asked a loud voice. "The fun is just getting started!"

The Head in the Door

Danny turned to see who was talking to him. Poking out of a door the size of a school notebook was a boy's head. He had a heap of fuzzy carrot-coloured hair and freckles across his cheeks. His mouth was so wide it looked like his face was cracked in two.

"Come on," he said, "What are you waiting for?"

"I can't fit in there," answered Danny. He walked until his feet were beside the door where the boy's face was sticking out. "It's too small."

"Oh, don't be such a nincompoop," the boy laughed, twisting his head to look up at Danny's face. "They just want us to think we can't get in. But we can! Just try it."

"Then let me see you get through it. Come to this side," Danny said.

The freckled head laughed so hard it shook.

"You want *moi* to come to you? Well, I could do that, but once I'm out, I may not get us back in, which is where we really want to be. You see, these little doors are a lot like recess. You've got to get out while you have the chance. If you dilly-dally to finish up spelling, clean your desk, put on your coat, then right when you're ready to have fun… DING-A-LING-A-LING-A-LING-A-LING. Bell rings, recess ends, and you're back at your desk doing math and waiting for the next chance to play. We don't know when this door will open again. Could be in an hour, could be in a day."

"You mean the door might disappear once you're through?"

"Ding-ding-ding!" the boy replied. "Young brilliant sir, your answer is correct!"

Jingo, who had been standing back several paces, piped in, "I told you. You can't come back the way you went in. Don't do it!"

The red-haired boy stretched his neck to get a look at Jingo and gasped.

"Get away from that virus!" he yelled.

"What?" said Danny as he moved away from Jingo.

"I'm not a virus!" Jingo said.

"He'll infect you!" the boy continued, "He's contagious. Don't touch him!"

"No, no," Jingo cried. "I'm safe. I'm safe. Really. Please, Danny, don't listen to him."

"How do I know you're telling the truth?" Danny asked.

Jingo dropped to his knees and cried. Blue tears splashed around Danny's feet.

"Oh please, believe me," he sobbed. "I haven't had a friend in so long. I'm not contagious. I promise. I'm not contagious. Please, don't leave me! You're my only friend."

Danny was moved by his friend's pleas. He remembered a couple years back when all his friends had turned against him for no reason and shut him out of the Booger Club. He and Harold (the class fish) had been the only grade one boys not allowed in. That night, he'd mined his nose for the best gem he could dig up. The next morning he'd brought in a nugget so big and shiny that even the girls fought over it. He became a member for life after that. But he never forgot how lonely and miserable he felt that one day.

"It's okay. I believe you," Danny said.

"All right," the head floating outside the small doorway called out. "Enough sniffles. It's time for fun! Now let's get this party started!"

The words of Danny's mom suddenly popped into his mind. **It's not safe**. He pushed the words around his head like a piece of broccoli on his dinner plate. How did she always know what was good for him? She didn't. He could make up his own mind once in a while. Her voice grew softer … *It's not safe — it's not safe — it's not safe — it's not safe* — until it was only a whisper.

"I don't know," Danny said, "My mom says it's dangerous over there."

The red-headed boy rolled his eyes and sighed, "Of course she did. Parents say that to make sure you don't have any fun. Think about it. They sit around drinking hot mud-coloured water and read huge pieces of paper covered with thousands of words that are too hard to read."

"The newspaper. Yuck," Danny agreed.

"My point is their life is D-U-L-L. Dull! Why would they want you to have fun when all they ever get is responsibility. In fact, you can't help but feel a little sorry for them."

Danny nodded his head. Parents did have it a bit tough.

"But don't waste your time worrying about them. You need to have fun when you get the chance. And all that talk about safety? Pchaw! Gobbledygook. Look at me. I'm a kid just like you. Do I look hurt?"

"Well, no," answered Danny.

"It's so much fun over here!" he cried, "But hey, if you're happy playing the same old kiddie games, then fine. See you later."

He ducked his head and disappeared behind the wall.

"I said, see you later," the voice floated out.

Danny had to think fast. He really wanted to try new games.

"Bye-bye!" the voice wandered out again.

I'm no chicken, thought Danny. Sure, my mom thinks it's dangerous, but jeez, what does she know? *It's not safe. It's not safe...* They're just games, after all. And with that, her words were tossed right out of his head.

"Wait!" Danny called.

The head popped back out the door. "Yes?"

"What's your name?"

"Desmond. What's yours?"

"Danny. And this is Jingo." Jingo nodded.

"Well, then," Desmond opened the crack across his face to form a smile. "Now that we're all friends, what are you waiting for? Let's go!"

Danny looked at Jingo and shrugged. "See? Desmond is a kid, just like me."

"Appearances aren't what they seem around here," Jingo whispered so that Desmond couldn't hear. "Be careful."

"I will," Danny promised, but he was growing tired of Jingo's lectures.

Danny lowered to his hands and knees and

crawled toward the small opening. How on earth would he get through such a tiny door? He leaned toward the floor and stuck his head through first then shoved his shoulders against the door's frame. Although stiff at first, the opening softened like dough and moulded to Danny's body so that it was just big enough to squirm through. Jingo stopped outside the door.

"Aren't you coming, too?" Danny asked.

Jingo looked at Danny then gazed at the world he'd be leaving behind. He nodded his head slowly.

"Yes. I'm coming."

Through the Wall

When Danny stood up, he covered his ears to muffle the loud noises swirling around him. In one area was hundreds of towers made up of huge boxes stacked one on top of the other. Some of the towers were so crooked that Danny wondered how they even stayed up. On each side of every box was a movie screen that played videos over and over again. They showed people singing, talking, dancing, hitting, crying, crawling, cooking, and anything else that a normal person (or not so normal person) could do. It was like watching a never-ending stream of bad movies.

In another area, a glowing white paper draped to the ground like a massive waterfall. Black shapes dropped like rain onto the bottom of the paper where they magically turned into letters. The letters slid around until they formed words and then flew to the top of the glowing paper where they joined thousands of sentences. Danny squinted his eyes as he tried to read some of the words, but then stopped himself. Reading was for books, not computers. Why would anyone want to read from a computer when there were so many more interesting things to do? Danny rubbed his eyes. This wasn't what he expected. Where were all the cool games that Desmond promised?

Suddenly one of the towers toppled over with a shattering clatter of breaking glass and screeching metal. Jingo grabbed hold of Danny's leg. Danny gripped Desmond's arm. Desmond giggled crazily as he watched the crash like it was some action movie.

"What was that?" Danny asked when it was over.

"A site crashed. Happens all the time," Desmond answered. "Cool, huh?"

Danny nodded his head silently. He wasn't used to that sort of thing and didn't want Desmond to know that it scared him.

"You can let go of my arm now," Desmond said, shaking his arm off.

"Oh right, sorry."

Danny looked down at Jingo. He unwrapped himself from Danny's leg and smiled weakly at him. Danny was relieved to see he wasn't the only terrified one.

"Time for some fun!" Desmond called as he led them through a wide brown door. They entered a jungle where tall trees with leaves as big as boats crowded over the boys. The chaos from outside faded away and was replaced by the calls of animals echoing throughout the forest.

"This place is creepy," said Jingo quietly. "We should go back to the wall, don't you think?"

"What do you guys think?" Desmond called proudly over his shoulder.

Danny patted Jingo on the head. "It's just a game," he whispered, "We'll go back right after this game. What do you think of that?"

"Great," Jingo announced loudly.

"I knew you'd love it!" Desmond yelled to Jingo. "Have a banana!" He leapt onto a tree then flung his body like a rubber band from branch to branch.

Danny reached for a low branch and climbed. Halfway up the tree he grabbed a twine and swung through the forest. The screams, hoots, and twitters of wild animals grew louder. A tremor of fear mixed with excitement ran through Danny's body.

"Watch out for the chimps!" yelled Desmond from somewhere up ahead.

"What do you mean?" Danny called back. He was about to pass Desmond's warning on to Jingo who was struggling somewhere in the forest behind him, but a long hairy hand landed on Danny's shoulder and dragged him down the twine.

His hands burned as he tried to slow his drop. He turned to see his attacker—a gorilla with two black eyes as big as tennis balls and a mouth with long yellow fangs. He counted six of them as the wide mouth leaned in to chomp on his neck.

"Aaaaaaaaaaah!" Danny screamed.

He stretched out his hand. It caught a branch and stopped his fall. The ape dropped off his back. Danny swung his legs onto the tree limb and lifted himself up. Far ahead, he saw Desmond pulling banana bunches from the trees and pummelling gorillas that got in his way. That's when Danny realized the bananas gave him power to swing faster and beat off chimps. That should be easy!

Danny leapt to another tree and reached for a

banana, but missed. A gorilla hugged his waist and together they fell through the air while twigs cracked around them. He pulled a bunch of bananas. A burst of strength pumped through his veins and with a backward flick of his head, he knocked the beast in the face. It fell away just before Danny crashed to the ground. He scrambled up a tree trunk and looked for Desmond. He eventually found him resting on a branch high above the forest floor, peeling a banana and laughing at Danny.

"Boy, you've got a lot of learning to do," Desmond said to Danny when he reached him.

"You could have helped me out a bit."

"Come on. If you want me to hold your hand like your mommy, then you should have stayed at home. This is for big boys."

Danny pouted. He was only asking for a little help. Where was Jingo anyway? Danny looked around him.

"I guess your little virus didn't make it," Desmond said. "Let's go to the next game!"

"My name's Jingo and I'm not a virus," a voice rang out, "I would appreciate it if you'd please stop saying that."

"Jingo!" Danny exclaimed, "You made it!"

"Were you going to leave without me?" Jingo asked quietly.

"Of course not," Danny answered.

"We were just hanging like a couple of wet towels," Desmond agreed. "Don't be so blue, Jingo-loo. We would have hung out a bit longer to see if you made it."

He scratched his chin where there was a scruffy mound of what looked like brown hair.

"But Danny doesn't want you slowing him down," Desmond muttered.

"Oh, I don't mind," Danny patted Jingo on the head. Then he turned to Desmond and pointed at his face.

"What's that on your chin?" he asked.

"Huh?" Desmond mumbled. "Oh, it's just dirt. I'll wash it off later."

It looked like hair to Danny. But that didn't make any sense. Boys don't grow hair on their face. Jingo shot Danny a knowing look.

Danny shrugged. His Aunt Lucy had a brown moustache (she coloured it white sometimes), so maybe it wasn't that weird that a boy could have a

beard. He didn't feel like explaining that to Jingo, though. Danny followed Desmond down the tree and out of the jungle with Jingo trailing him.

"I thought we were going back to the wall," said Jingo from behind.

"Uh, well, how about one more game?" Danny asked. "I think I can do better on the next game, don't you?"

"That depends on the game," Jingo replied.

"Well, you don't know anything, anyways," Danny said in a huff. He planned on being the best player ever. Even if it took a hundred thousand bazillion more games. And no one, including Jingo, would get in his way.

"Are you coming or not?" asked Danny impatiently.

"Yes, if you don't mind. I'm coming," answered Jingo.

Deal of a Lifetime

The trio stepped out of the game and walked across a bridge that led to a flea market. It was much better than the one his parents dragged him to last summer, where they lifted one old piece of junk after another admiring its dents and cracks that gave it "personality." They'd even showed Danny a lopsided metal car attached to some dirty string, "Look Danny!" they'd said, "This is the kind of toy your granddad used to play with!" Like, wow! Danny had thought, no wonder it was so rusted. Geez, kids must have been really bored in the olden days.

In this place, Danny and his friends were surrounded by fantastical inventions displayed on shiny black wagons that whizzed around on wheels. Attached to each wagon was a long copper handle that the seller pulled from one direction to another, searching for buyers. Together, all those wagons created such a commotion that Danny expected another eruption like the one he'd seen earlier. When that didn't happen, the boys gathered some courage and stepped into the rushing market, dodging wagons and chasing those gadgets and gizmos that most interested them. One glittering contraption caught Danny's eye. The cart slowed down and Danny stared in wonder as he moved closer to it.

"You want it," a sharp voice commanded.

Danny nodded without looking up. I want it, he thought. I want it.

It was an amazing thingamabob that was like nothing he'd ever seen. It was made up of glassy tubes that glowed as they twisted like tangled snakes into a different shape every few seconds. First it was a football, then a guitar, then a robot, then a…

"It's a tizzeedooder," the voice explained.

Danny looked up. A large woman with cheeks that hung like pancakes on either side of her small lips stared at him through round eyes the colour of syrup. As she swayed her big belly toward him, her yellow skirt swung like a bell. Danny could almost hear it ding-dong.

"Every boy wants a tizzeedooder," she said as she lifted it from the wagon and handed it to Danny. As she did so, it made a magical chime of a hundred Christmas bells. Danny thought of gingerbread cookies and stockings full of treats. There was nothing in the world he wanted more than a tizzeedooder.

"Blow it," said the woman. "It's got all the bells and whistles."

Danny put his mouth to the end of one tube and blew. A tune as smooth as ice cream came out.

"So cool," Danny said. But what on earth would he ever do with a tizzeedooder? That thought jumped out of his head as quick as a cricket. *Who cares?* He just knew he had to have it.

"What use is it, please?" Jingo asked the woman.

"None of your friends will have a tizzeedooder," she said, her brown sugar eyes set on Danny.

"Excuse me, what's it for?" Jingo asked again.

"A tizzeedooder is what every boy needs," she spoke severely, as though she were a doctor explaining a flu shot.

"I want it!" blurted Danny.

"That's seventy-five dollars."

"I don't have seventy-five dollars."

"We take credit," she said, snatching the tiz-zeedooder from his hands.

"Uh, I don't have credit," said Danny. "What is credit?"

"Credit gets you something for nothing. It's very generous."

"Well, I have nothing," Danny said. "So, can I have it?"

The lady beamed. "You have nothing? Then credit is for you. Just fill out this form and soon you'll be buying all kinds of things for nothing." She pulled out of her skirt a small square piece of paper with a big 'X' where he needed to sign.

"You mean I can get this for free if I have credit?" Danny asked.

"Read the form. It explains that getting something now will cost you nothing for now (why wait till later if you can have it now?) But credit will want something back in the near future. Something a little more, that is, than the something you got for nothing unless you can give it back exactly what it asks for when it asks for it. Got it? Sign here."

"I'm confused," Danny confessed.

"You wouldn't be the first," said Desmond. He moved Danny and Jingo away from the woman as she flapped the form at them. "Don't bother with that. You'll find something better."

He led them to a wagon covered with bottles of different shapes and colours. The seller was long and curvy like a string of licorice. He dipped his head down to Danny's face.

"Hello-o-o-o-o, little boys." Two pointy ears stiffened on top of his head as he spoke. "Perhaps I can interest you in my potion called Kwickficks. One drink of it and you will be stronger than a hundred giants, speedier than a rocket, and smarter than a three-piece suit. What do you say?"

Visions of greatness paraded through Danny's mind. Win every race at recess! Ace every test without ever doing homework! Beat the highest video game score of all time! Gold medals and contracts for his own reality shows filled his head until it was bursting.

"Oh yeah!" Danny responded enthusiastically. "That would be awesome!"

Jingo nudged him. Danny leaned down so that his ear was next to Jingo's mouth.

"Please be careful," Jingo warned him. "There are no shortcuts to getting stronger, or faster, or smarter. It takes work. Not a gulp of medicine."

"How do you know?" Danny asked.

"Take a short cut and you cut yourself short," Jingo shrugged. "That's just the way it is."

Danny crossed his arms, "We'll see about that."

He turned his back on Jingo and grabbed Desmond's arm.

"I really want it!"

Desmond smiled, "I knew you would. Isn't it cool?"

"How can I buy it?"

Desmond cleared his throat, "Excuse me. My friend here would like your potion. But, uh, he has no money or credit. Can we make some sort of deal?"

The man purred like a kitten, and brushed off some invisible specks on the shoulders of his suit. He turned his eyes to Jingo and stared for a minute or two as a smile grew across his face.

"The virus," he purred, "I'll take the virus."

"I'm not a virus, sir," Jingo said.

"Yeah! He's not a virus," Danny argued. "He's my friend and you're not taking him."

The man sniffed. "Well then, no potion for you.

Come back to me when you have something to pay me with."

Danny shuffled his feet. Oh, how he wanted the potion. Perhaps Jingo could just stay with him for a while. Just until Danny could make enough money to buy him back.

"Jingo, buddy," Desmond held out his hands, "Come on. Why not do your friend a favour and hang out like a dude until Danny can buy you back. He'll just play one game, then we'll return."

Jingo shifted his eyes to Danny, "Is that really what you want? Do you really want me to stay here alone?"

Danny felt horrible about leaving Jingo, but he really, really wanted that potion.

"I'll just be gone for one game," Danny answered, "I promise I'll be back right after that." He turned to Desmond. "We can make money to buy him back, right?"

Desmond snapped his fingers. "Lickety-split, Dan-eroo!"

"See?" said Danny. "You don't have to worry. I'll be back before you know it."

"You promise?" Jingo asked.

"Promise!" Danny answered. He'd promised lots

of things to his mom and dad in the past. He'd promised to clean his room before dinner, to say thank-you whenever he got something, to stop giving his brother wedgies. He never actually kept his word on those things. But this time was different. He really meant it this time. And those other promises were just so hard to keep!

"All right, then," said Jingo. "I'll do it because you're my best friend."

"Thanks Jingo!" Danny was thrilled. He held out his hand to the man, "It's a deal. But he's just staying here until I return with money to pay for the potion. Got it?"

"Sure," the man answered as he handed Danny a small round glass bottle. A purple liquid swished inside of it. Danny popped off the lid and drank it in one gulp.

He stood there, waiting for something to happen. Anything. There was nothing.

"I don't feel anything," said Danny.

"It takes a minute," the man answered. He picked up Jingo and set him on his wagon. Jingo looked scared.

"It'll be okay, little Jingle," the man said. "I won't hurt you."

List of Promises I
can keep:

1) Eat my dessert every night.

2) Mess my bed every night.

3) Pretend to listen in class.

4) Share with my brother
when he's not around.

Danny looked at Jingo and felt a squeeze in his heart. "You won't forget me, will you?" Jingo asked.

"I promise I'll be back soon." He patted his blue friend's leg. "You're the best friend a boy could ever have!"

At that, Jingo smiled. "You mean it?"

"Yes, I really do."

"Ready now?" Desmond asked, "Let's go!"

A tingling started in his feet and quickly moved up his legs and across the rest of his body.

"You'd better go," the man advised, "Before it wears off!"

"What?" Danny exclaimed, "It wears off? You didn't tell me that!"

"It's all in the fine print." He pointed to a white label on the bottle about the size of a finger tip.

"I know the perfect game!" Desmond yelled as he ran ahead.

Danny waved good-bye to Jingo than hurried to catch up with Desmond.

Burst of Power

The tingling turned into painful pin pricks all over his body and Danny felt as powerless as ever. His legs were too weak to run and he had to slow down.

"I need to stop," Danny tried calling after Desmond, but he was too far ahead to hear. Just as he was about to fall to the ground, a hot burst of energy came from inside his stomach. It was sort of like the feeling Danny got when he was kicking a soccer goal. Like nothing could stop him!

"Yeah!" Danny hollered as the power spread to his arms and legs. He sprang straight up into the sky like a super sonic bouncy ball. While up there, he scanned the area below and spotted a cap of orange hair zooming through a commotion of wagons, videos, and pathways. Desmond!

Danny landed and charged ahead like a cheetah.

His feet barely touched the ground as he chased Desmond. I'll show him, thought Danny.

"Woo-hooooo!" He yelled as he sprang clear over Desmond's head.

"Hey, look at you!" Desmond laughed, "Wait up!"

They raced until Desmond stopped suddenly.

"This way," he pointed to a cave that appeared out of nowhere. They'd long ago passed the market where Jingo was waiting. Danny worried that they may be a long way from him now and getting back wouldn't be so easy.

"Now you're really going to see what you can do with those new powers," Desmond said.

Danny could hardly wait. He'd worry about Jingo later. Together they entered the cave and followed a dark tunnel that grew taller and wider the deeper they went until there were no walls at all.

"If you can play this game, you rock," Desmond winked.

He ran ahead, kicking up a swirl of red dust from the ground. Danny followed him, but got lost in the flying dust. He stood still and listened. He heard nothing. When the red storm settled, he saw only dark empty space. Is this some sort of a dumb joke?

Danny wondered. There's nothing to do! And where did Desmond go?

A rumbling erupted in the distance. It sounded like an earthquake, and as it grew louder, Danny grew jittery. Out of nowhere, a huge boulder barrelled toward him. He was so scared, he couldn't think about anything other than his sudden urge to pee his pants. The boulder was just a breath away! Finally he came to his senses and jumped out of the way.

A stampede of massive rocks followed, tumbling angrily toward him. He panicked. There was no way he could move fast enough! Then he remembered the Kwickficks potion and his courage returned. I can do this, he told himself. Danny jumped high over a boulder and zipped around another, and another. All around him the giant stones smashed together, exploding like popped corn.

"Come and get me!" he taunted the charging boulders. As if hearing him, a bunch of stones gathered together like an army and rushed at him.

"Mwa-ha-ha-haaaa," he laughed wickedly and jumped right on top of one of the boulders and rode it like a cowboy. He galloped along with it until SMASH... it rammed into another boulder and blew up. He flew with the explosion and landed feet first onto another racing rock.

"Yee-haaw!" whooped Danny, "Who's your daddy?"

He jumped rocks until nothing but rubble was left on the ground. That's when he noticed white circles swinging like hula hoops in the dark sky. Danny jumped up and hooked his fingers onto the closest hoop and flipped his body through it. Immediately the loop transformed into a bubble inside of which Danny sat as he floated up and up and up. Hundreds of hoops flapped like seagulls around him. Danny folded his arms behind his head and laid back for a short rest. Then POP! He dropped like an anchor and landed with a clank on the ground. He rubbed his solid butt. Good thing it's hard as glass in this world, or that woulda hurt b-a-a-a-a-ad! Looking up to figure out what had popped the bubble, he finally noticed tiny red darts shooting among the hula hoops. One of the sneaky little things had hit his bubble.

He jumped up and into another hoop. This time, he watched for the darts. POP! Danny was ready. He aimed his body for a flock of hoops and was soon floating peacefully again. Up, up, up he floated. And pop, pop, pop he fell. Eventually he rose higher and higher and the red dusty ground moved further away.

As he ascended into a pink-coloured sky, an unusual sound grew louder. *Shwow- shwow-shwow.* Danny looked up. He was headed into the middle of an asteroid belt! It looked like a huge snowball fight except, instead of white balls of fluff whizzing everywhere, they were enormous chunks of glittering rock.

One careened toward him. Danny squeezed his eyes shut. POP! The bubble disappeared and Danny landed on the speeding asteroid. CLANK went his rear-end, again. Danny flattened his body against the rock as it dashed through the other blasting stones. A meteoroid shot toward him. He shut his eyes and pushed out his arms, not sure how that would do him any good. Then POW! The rock slammed into his hands and exploded into blue flames. Danny opened his eyes. Wow, he thought, did I do that? He jumped to his feet and swayed his hips.

"Oh yeah, I did it! Who's the best? Who's the best? It's Danny. It's Danny," he sang as another meteoroid bounced off his head.

An asteroid flew by and Danny jumped on it, landing on his feet. Awesome! He leaped again. But this time his legs buckled and he stumbled onto his hands and knees. They were tingling again. He tried to get himself back up but he was suddenly too tired to move.

His asteroid tipped to one side. Danny tried to grip the edge and hang on, but he slid right off and fell past the pink sky, past the glowing hoops, and Bam! Into the red dust. The boulders were rolling toward him but this time, Danny couldn't move.

"Help!" he cried.

He felt his legs lift then his entire body dragged swiftly across the ground.

"It's over! I'm not going to make it," he sobbed, "I want my Mommy! Help me!"

Danny's legs dropped to the ground with a thunk.

"You're fine," said an annoyed voice. "And your mommy isn't here, big guy."

Danny opened one eye. Desmond stood over him, shaking his head. They were out of the game.

"I knew that," Danny snorted as he laughed. "I knew that was you."

"Sure you did."

Danny lifted his head and tried to stand up, but his belly ached.

"My stomach," whined Danny. "I'm going to be sick."

"It's wearing off," Desmond said.

"What?"

"The potion. It's done."

"That's it? I barely got to finish one game! That's what I gave Jingo up for?"

"It was worth it! You reached the highest level in one of the toughest games here!"

"I did? That's cool." In that case, Danny thought, it had been worth it. But now he had to get back to his blue buddy.

"We need to get Jingo," Danny said.

"What's the rush?"

Danny stared at him in disbelief. They promised Jingo they would return as soon as they'd finished their game. He looked closely at his red-headed friend. Something just didn't seem right about him. Maybe it was his eyes — the way they knocked about in his sockets like pin balls. Why couldn't he just look at me straight like every other kid?

"He's waiting for us. That's the rush," Danny answered.

"Bla-a-a-ah!" Desmond frowned. For just a second, Danny thought he saw a slithery tongue shoot out from his friend's mouth. He shook his head. It must be his imagination.

"No more games until we buy Jingo back," stated Danny.

Desmond shrugged. "Well then, let's earn some money."

Make Them Like You

"What do I do?" Danny asked.

"You have to be funny," Desmond said dully.

"Funny?" Danny scrunched his face.

"Funny, like ha-ha. Not funny looking!"

Danny sneered and stuck out his tongue. "All right. Be funny. But how will that get me money?"

"The more people like you, the more they want to see you. The more they want to see you, the more they want to spend their money to keep seeing you."

"But how does being funny help me do that?"

"Everybody loves to laugh!" Desmond threw his arms into the air. "It's called entertainment. And it makes them feel great! People will pay to feel great!"

"Uh-huh," Danny said, tapping his toe on the ground. "Make them laugh. Hmmmm. How will anyone know if I'm funny? There's nobody even here."

"If you're funny, word will spread like peanut butter. The crowds will come when they hear about it. Trust me." Desmond gave the thumbs up.

Danny stood there scratching his head.

"That's not funny," said Desmond.

"I'm not trying to be funny. I'm thinking!"

Danny stuck his tongue out and crossed his eyes.

"What are you doing?" asked Desmond.

"I'm making a funny face!"

"More like an ugly face."

"Okay, I got one," Danny cleared his throat. "A teacher tells her class to sit down. One kid stays standing. She says to him 'why don't you sit down?' He answers 'my butt is broken.' She says 'it looks perfectly fine to me, young man.' He says, 'but it's cracked!"

"Ha!" Desmond laughed, "Good one. Got more?"

"That's all I got."

"We're in trouble."

Danny's shoulders slumped. "What am I going to do? You said it'd be easy to get Jingo back. This is not easy!"

"Just forget about Jingo," Desmond urged him. "He's a virus."

Danny stamped his foot. "I will not forget about him. And he's not a virus."

"He is a virus."

"Is not!"

"Is too!"

"Take it back!"

Desmond put his hands on his hips. "Make me!"

Danny lunged at him. Desmond ducked and Danny stumbled to the ground.

"Who taught you how to fight? Your baby sister?" Desmond teased.

Danny felt his face redden. "Take it back!"

"Make me!"

Danny jumped to his feet and bulldozed head first into Desmond's stomach. He crumpled to the ground. Danny sat on his back and wrapped his arm around Desmond's neck, forcing him into a headlock.

"Take it back!"

"No!" Desmond yanked Danny's arm off his neck and flipped him over his red head. Danny landed on his back. "Ooph!"

Desmond jumped to his feet, stepped back a few paces, then sprang into the air and body slammed him.

"Take that!"

"Ooooh!"

"Get up! Dude!" a stranger's voice called out. "Yeah! Get him!" another voice cheered.

Danny and Desmond lifted their heads. There was a crowd of boys and girls circling them. Their eyes were bright, their cheeks flushed. Some of them threw punches into the air.

"Don't stop!" A kid with a ponytail coming out of her ball cap yelled. She tossed a gold coin onto the ground near them. Others followed. A smattering of coins tinkled to the ground.

"You did it!" Desmond said. "They love you!"

"But they're not laughing. I thought I had to make them laugh!"

"You're entertaining them. That's all that matters. Lots of people like punches as much as punch lines."

Desmond lifted his fist and pounded Danny in the stomach. "We gotta give them what they want!"

"Oh!" Danny had the wind knocked out of him for a second. He shoved Desmond off him and they rolled around on the ground as the kids cheered.

He pinned Desmond to the ground and stuck his knee into his neck. Then he lifted one of Desmond's arms and twisted.

"Ow!" yelled Desmond. "Stop!"

"Not until you say you're sorry!" He twisted it harder.

"More.. More… More…" Chanted the crowd.

"I'm sorry!" yelled Desmond. "NOT!"

Danny dropped Desmond's arm and pulled his own fist back past his ear. Desmond was really going to get it now. He held his clenched hand in the air.

"I said say sorry!" Danny demanded through clenched teeth.

Desmond laughed. "Do it! Hit me! Do it!"

"Hit him… Hit him… Hit him…" the kids chanted.

Danny's body shook with anger. He was ready to pound him. It would be so easy. Jingo's blue face suddenly appeared in his head. Was this going to help save his friend?

"Hit him… Hit him… Hit him!"

Danny shot his fist down. Cra-a-a-a-ack! The floor broke in two under his fist where he slammed it. Danny clutched his throbbing hand.

"Why didn't you hit me?" Desmond asked. "That's what the crowd wanted."

Danny climbed off Desmond. "Who cares what

they want? It's not right. I don't want to hit you. Aren't we supposed to be friends?"

He stood up and offered a hand to Desmond.

"That's it?" A loud-mouthed boy from the crowd yelled.

"Booooo!" howled the fans. "Boooooo!"

Danny picked up the coins from the ground. Both his pockets were heavy with metal. The crowd disappeared.

"We have enough now," Danny said. "Let's get back to Jingo."

"I know a short cut," said Desmond.

"Oh great."

"What did one pilot say to another?"

"What?"

"Ready. Jet. Go."

Before Danny had a chance to say 'what a stinker' a dark green jet landed beside them.

Explosions and Lightning and Thunder, Oh My!

Desmond climbed into the jet and buckled himself in. He waved as the canopy lowered over him.

"Just fly straight!" He yelled through the glass as the plane lifted off.

"Wait...!" Danny ran to the jet but it flew off before he reached it.

Another plane arrived. Danny had no choice but to follow Desmond. He climbed into the cockpit and stared at an instrument panel that had more blinking lights than a Christmas tree. There was one lever in the very center. A glowing green button read **Ready for Takeoff**. Danny pushed it and a seatbelt slid across his chest. Straps closed around his ankles. He grasped the lever.

"I guess this is it," said Danny. His heart pounded against his chest. He'd never flown in a plane before, much less piloted one. He didn't know if he could do it.

Danny sucked in a nervous breath then exhaled slowly and counted backwards from ten. His mom had taught him to do that whenever he was upset or scared. Ten, nine, eight, seven, six, five... Oh, forget it! Just go for it! He pulled the lever down and blasted into the clouds.

"Whoa!" yelled Danny as he tried to steady his plane. It dipped, flipped, and flopped like a roller coaster ride. Danny gripped the lever with both hands and held fast until the jet straightened.

"That rocked!" Danny cried out, "I want to do that again!"

He noticed a row of buttons. Each one had on it a different design.

Curious, Danny hit the first one. His jet propelled straight into the sky and flipped upside down in a loop then back to where he started.

"Wow!" yelled Danny, "that was sick!"

He pushed the second button. It sent his plane

spinning like a drill through the clouds until Danny felt his macaroni lunch galloping from his tummy back to his mouth. The jet steadied just as a noodle reached his tongue. His finger hovered above the buttons as he decided which one to try next. *Eeny, meeny, miny, mo… Catch a tiger by the toe… when it…* suddenly a shadow fell over him. He looked up to find an airplane as big as five school buses flying right above him.

"What is that?"

Just then, he heard a loud *thooooooooooo*. A bomb! And, it was going to hit him! Danny had to get out of the way! He scanned the panel for a button to push…

…and pressed *Fast Forward*. The plane shot forward and dodged the bomb. An airplane that had been beneath him was not so lucky—it blasted into a ball of fire. The force of the explosion pummelled Danny's plane toward the ground. He lowered the lever to lift the nose of the jet up, but it did not stop his free fall.

"I'm gonna crash!" he screamed hysterically, "I'm gonna crash!"

The jet lifted just before hitting the ground and headed back up into the sky. Phew, that was a close one, he thought.

He barely had time to catch his breath when he noticed two gold and black aircrafts zooming toward him. Bullets sprayed all around him. Ta-ta-ta-ta-ta-ta-ta. The tip of one of his wings caught fire. Danny aimed at the jet closest to him and shot a missile. Bulls-eye! It hit his attacker and sent him diving to the ground. The second jet swooped up over him, then made a U-turn and shot bullets at him from behind. Black smoke trailed his other wing. He'd been hit again!

Danny lifted the nose of his plane and rode it like a rocket straight up past the clouds. Then he levelled his jet and darted across the sky until he was above the shooting plane, and dropped a bomb. **BOOM!**

"Pa-Chow!" Danny exclaimed as the plane fell. "Sweet hit."

Now he had to find Desmond. Why does that guy always disappear on me? And what way should I be flying anyway? There was one thing he knew for certain. He was lost. Miles above ground and surrounded by enemy war planes, Danny had no idea where he was supposed to go.

The sky turned grey, then black, and freezing rain hammered his flier. Lightning flashed and thunder rumbled so loud that his bones trembled. He thought about Jingo's warnings. He was right. They shouldn't have gone through the wall. This is no place for a boy. Why didn't he listen? At home, his mom said she would protect him. Who would protect him now? A tear formed in the corner of his eye, but before it fell, he heard a crackle over his speaker.

"Danny… Come in, Danny."

"Desmond! Where are you?"

"You're almost out of it," he said. "Just go straight!"

Danny wiped the puddles in his eyes. In the distance he saw sunny skies. He swerved around lightning bolts, never taking his eyes off that patch of blue sky ahead.

"I'm almost out of it," he said to calm himself. "Just keep flying straight."

But something didn't seem right. The plane was dipping to the ground. Danny pulled the lever to straighten the body of the plane, but it did nothing. The lights on his instrument panel flashed and the needle on his fuel gauge pointed to empty.

"I'm going down!" Danny yelled.

"You're almost here," Desmond replied.

"No. I'm out of fuel. I'm gonna crash!"

"Eject! Eject!" Desmond yelled through the speaker.

"What?"

"Eject out of the plane! Hit the eject button!"

Danny found the button.

He said a quick prayer, fastened his helmet, and then pushed the button. He shot out of the plane like a spit ball and watched his jet fall and crash to the ground. A parachute puffed over his head and gently carried him to safety. Danny pulled the parachute off his head and found Desmond standing beside him with a huge grin.

A Pitiful Boy

"You made it!" Desmond croaked in a voice that sounded more like a tree frog than a boy.

"Yeah. Piece of cake," Danny answered weakly. "What's wrong with your voice?"

"Ahem..." He coughed. "I must have caught a cold up in the air."

Danny stood up after unfastening his straps and noticed the top of his head was barely past Desmond's shoulders. Hadn't they been the same size when they first met?

"You're taller," Danny said suspiciously.

"Don't be jealous. You'll grow too!" Desmond taunted, "It's called a growth spurt. You should try it some time — Shorty!"

"Hey, don't call me that! And I'm not jealous," Danny said defensively. He straightened his back and lifted his heels off the ground so that he was closer to Desmond's height. Maybe he hadn't grown that much after all, Danny reasoned.

He didn't trust Desmond any more. He was nice one minute and nasty the next. In fact, Danny didn't even like him. Friends don't leave friends every time a game starts. And Desmond sure didn't give a bird's turd about Jingo being taken away. As soon as they found Jingo he would leave Desmond. But for now, he had to stay with him.

"Well, here we are!" exclaimed Desmond. Wagons rolled around them.

"We made it!" said Danny, relieved. They ran through the sellers searching for the man with the potions. They ran one way, then the other. Up one aisle, down another. Through alleys, across bridges. But the man with the pointy ears was nowhere to be found.

"Where is he?" cried Danny. "He was supposed to wait. I said I'd be back!"

Desmond shrugged and whistled as his eyes rolled in circles.

"You know something, don't you?" Danny asked. He grabbed Desmond's shoulders. "Tell me! Where is Jingo?"

Desmond pulled Danny's hands off. "All right. He's probably been sold to the Disinfectors. It's too late."

"The what?"

"The Disinfectors… they capture viruses and then take them apart so that they can't spread their diseases to anyone else. They would have paid a lot for Jingo."

"What?" Danny cried. "How could you do this? Jingo is my friend!"

"He's a virus! We can't have viruses running around."

"He's not a virus! He told me so."

"Do you believe everything you hear?"

Danny glared at Desmond. "I shouldn't, should I?" he answered. "How do I know you are who you say you are?"

Desmond took a step back. "Hey, I'm your buddy. You wanted me to show you a good time. I've done that. You wanted that potion. I got it for you. You were the one who left Jingo behind. Not me!"

"We need to help Jingo. Please help me find him."

"It's impossible," Desmond argued. "He's gone. He's probably been disinfected already. There's nothing we can do." Desmond shrugged, "It's too late."

"Noooooo," Danny cried. He turned from Desmond and ran. He ran and ran and ran as tears streamed down his cheeks. How could I do this to my friend? I'm a horrible boy! Why did I have to go through the wall? Why didn't I listen to Jingo? Why didn't I listen to my mom? I'm bad, bad, bad.

He reached the end of the road. To his left was a sign that read Piteemee. The sad voices of boys and girls whining like sirens about their troubled lives filled the darkened pathway. "It's not fair... I aimed the ball at his hands not his teeth... I couldn't wait for a toilet... I thought dirty clothes were supposed to go under my bed...He wanted me to kick him there..."

Danny nodded. He understood them. It was tough being a kid. A girl with two long pony tails wandered ahead of him. She turned around and waved him in.

"Life is so unfair, isn't it?" she asked him when he caught up to her.

"It's so unfair," Danny agreed. "It's not my fault I came through the wall. My mom should have warned me more. Why did Jingo agree to stay with the potions man? It's his fault. Anyway, Desmond made me do it. It's not my fault."

"It's never our fault," she explained. Complaints spat out of her mouth like cherry pits—one after another after another. Danny nodded his head, but was not listening. He had his own problems. He hurried past her, reciting his own list of miseries.

"Now I'll never find Jingo. And I'll never get back home. And I'll be stuck in this computer world forever. Ooooh! Why me?" He remembered all the horrible things that had ever happened to him in his long life of ten years. Like the time he had to share his new remote control dinosaur with his brother. And when he was sent to his room at his own birthday party because he said he didn't like a gift (a boy Barbie – come on!) And why, oh why did he have to make his bed every morning. It just got messy again!

"Life is so unfair," he moaned.

As he muttered about his unhappy life, he walked down a steep, bumpy path. At the bottom he saw boys and girls sitting in a grey room whining to one another. He wanted to join them so he could share his own sad story. Surely, no one's life was as bad as his.

"Blah, blah, blah, blah," their voices carried up to Danny. "Blah, blah, blah, blah," agreed Danny. "Blah, blah, blah, blah... Blah, blah, blah, blah."

A tiny voice cried inside Danny's head. ""You won't forget me, will you?"

Danny stopped. Jingo! I have to save Jingo. How could I waste so much time feeling sorry for myself when my friend needs help?

Danny knew what he needed to do. He turned from the whining kids and climbed back up. His legs ached but he did not stop until he reached the top. He'd made it. Now he had to find Jingo.

Gooligans

"There you are!" Desmond greeted Danny. "I didn't think you'd ever get out of that place. Most kids don't."

Danny turned up his nose. "What do you care?"

"Danny-o. We're buddies, remember? And I've been thinking."

"Uh-huh."

"There is a way to find out what happened to Jingo."

"Really? That's great!"

Desmond cocked his head to the side. "Only problem is, they're not always truthful."

"What do you mean *they?* Who are not always truthful?"

Desmond opened his mouth to answer but a loud whirring sound interrupted him. He turned around to see a gang of boys and girls wheeling toward them. As they drew closer, Danny realized they weren't regular kids, like him. They had no feet. Their legs were attached to wheels instead. Way cool, thought Danny, who had always thought walking was the worst way of getting around.

Their noses were shaped like small beaks and their eyes were sharp as an eagle's glare. Although they were the same size as Danny, they seemed more like adults. Perhaps it was the way they stood so tall and straight. Or maybe it was because they had that certain know-it-all look that Danny only ever noticed in parents and teachers. The unblinking stare and tight lips that meant 'I know you're lying, so 'fess up now or you're really in for it.'

Normally that look scared him (like when his mom found old green beans and broccoli bits from dinner in all his pant pockets.) But this time Danny was happy to see it. It meant they might know about Jingo.

Leading the gang was a small but sturdy guy whose shoulders jutted out like bricks on either side of his thick neck. His mouth was set in a straight line and he stared harshly at Danny as he screeched to a halt in front of him. His body wobbled back to front until he steadied himself on his wheel. Danny took a step back but Desmond stood right behind him and forced him to stay put.

"Ask about Jingo," he whispered.

"What?" Danny whispered back, "Who are they?"

"Hey Danny, what's up?" the leader asked casually.

"Uh, hi," Danny answered. "You know my name?"

The guy laughed in a way that didn't really sound like he was amused. The gang laughed along with him. Danny relaxed and joined them. Suddenly the snickering stopped and only Danny continued to giggle loudly.

"You don't think I'm *stupid*? Do you?" the leader asked.

Danny was stunned to silence. "Do I think you're, uh, s-s-stupid? No. No."

"That's good. Because for a second there, it sounded like you didn't think I knew everything there is to know. Do you not know that I know everything about everything here?" he said in a way that didn't really sound like a question.

"Oh, Yes. Great!" Danny nodded his head vigorously. "And, who are you?"

"I'm one of the gooligans," he answered, straightening his chest and pushing his shoulders back. "You got a question? Get a gooligan. We got the answers."

"Gooligans?" Danny repeated.

Desmond whispered in his ear, "It's true. They do know everything."

Danny felt a leap in his stomach. They would know about Jingo!

"But they lie," continued Desmond. "It's not their fault. They just don't know what's true and what's false. That's your job to figure out. They just pass on what they learn."

"Oh great," muttered Danny.

"So what do you want to know?" A big girl in a red dress rode up beside the leader. "Wait. I know. Help with your hygiene, right? Bad gas?

"No-o-o-o," said Danny, blushing.

"Body odour? I can help you with that."

"Me? No!"

"Long toe nails."

"Uh…"

"I knew it! First off, no more trimming those nasty toenails with your teeth," she told him.

I don't bite my toenails much.
Doesn't everyone bite their toenails?

"Why not?" Danny asked, then he shook his head. "Wait! No. That's not why I need help!"

"Of course. Bad breath." She covered her nose with one hand.

"No."

"You can't help it! It's a *condition*."

"No!" Danny shook his head. "I don't care about hygiene... I mean... I do, but that's not why I'm here. It's Jingo. I want to know about Jingo. Does anyone know what happened to him?"

A gooligan smaller than the others wheeled to the front and was about to talk, but the leader spoke over him.

"I know about Jingo. He's gone to the recycler center, like every virus. He's probably already been tossed in. You'll never see him again."

"That can't be right! Why would they do that? He wouldn't harm anyone. And he's not a virus. He told me so!" Danny crossed his arms and glared at him. "You lie."

"I lie?" he asked. "Well, when I'm really, really sleepy, I do. We all need to once in a while."

Danny started to protest but the smallest gooligan spoke up.

"Um, uh, can I say something?" He raised a finger.

"What do you have to add? I told him everything," said the leader with irritation in his voice.

"Jingo was put in a bus to the disinfectant facility," the smallest gang member continued. "They're doing tests on him to learn about what kind of virus he is. Then they will dispose of him."

"Dispose of him? What do you mean dispose of him?" Danny asked.

"Destroy him. Viruses must be destroyed. That's the rule."

"But he's not a virus!"

The other gooligans laughed.

"Poor Danny," said the leader, "We've all been fooled by a virus at one time or another."

"Well," the smallest of the group spoke softly. "There is a chance that Jingo is not a virus."

"Yes! That's right. He's not, he's not. I need to find him!" Danny pleaded. "Help me find him, please!"

The leader tossed a red ball toward Danny. It bounced at his feet.

"Follow the path to the recycler. That is where he is. If he's still alive."

The ball bounced into the distance leaving a red path behind it for Danny to follow. The kinder gooligan placed a blue ball at Danny's feet and rolled it in the opposite direction. A bright blue path blazed behind the ball as it rolled onward.

"This is the way to the disinfectant facility. You'll find him there." Then he lifted right off the ground and swayed like a kite in the air, before disappearing into the distance. Danny was astounded. They could fly, too!

"If you follow that blue path, you're following a dream. Stick to reality and follow the red ball. That's where you'll find him, whatever's left of him," said the leader.

As the gang revved off, some on ground and others into the sky, Danny pondered which way to go. Only one of them was right. But which one? He looked at the red path. If Jingo was at the recycler, then it was probably too late to save him. Or maybe it wasn't. What if Danny got there just in time to stop him from being thrown in? Then he should take the red path, just in case that was the truth.

But what if he was at the disinfectant facility? Danny looked at the blue path. Danny could try to get there before they disposed of him. And if Jingo is not a virus, he could be let out! Danny rubbed his eyes. Making decisions was hard work. He shivered. The air around him was growing colder.

"Well?" Desmond asked.

Danny stood tall and turned toward one path. "Hope. I will follow my hope."

He stepped onto the blue path.

Follow the Blue Path

Danny paid no attention to the sights around him as he followed the path. Sounds rang in his ears... Smashing games, screeching music, chattering voices. None of them interested him anymore. He cared only about finding Jingo. He'd even forgotten about Desmond trailing behind him. But his loud muttering eventually forced Danny out of his own deep thoughts.

"Walka-walka-walka. Ticka-tocka-ticka-tocka," Desmond rattled on like a train.

Danny turned around. Desmond's feet shuffled along with his head hanging low.

"*What are you saying?*" Danny asked.

"Huh?" his head popped up.

"That noise. It's weird and totally annoying!"

"Was I saying something?"

Danny rolled his eyes. "Duh, yeah! Can you stop?"

"I'm sorry, sorry. It's just when I'm hungry-hungry-hungry, I talka-talka-talka." He wiped away a stream of drool on his chin with the back of his hand. "I'll try to stoppa-stoppa."

This seemed odd to Danny, but he knew first-hand what hunger can do to a person. His mom called him Grizzly when he was starving because she claimed he growled like a bear until he got food in his stomach. He couldn't imagine what she'd say if he muttered on like a crazy person before every dinner. He walked faster, thankful that Desmond had quieted down. The sooner he got to the end of the path, the better.

He rounded past a hill. Just ahead was an orange one-storey building that had no windows, just one tall black door right in its center. The blue line ended there. For such a horrible place, Danny didn't find it scary looking at all.

Surrounding the disinfectant facility was a tall fence made up of long white sticks connected by silver criss-crossed poles, shaped like the letter 'x'. Atop each stick was a large white oval-shaped ball with strange markings. Danny couldn't wait to bang on that door and demand they free Jingo. Nothing could stop him now! He marched to the fence and grabbed two of the criss-crossed poles to swing under to get the other side. The silver poles moved then grabbed Danny by the waist and lifted him into the air.

"Desmond! Help!" Danny screamed.

One of the balls on top of the sticks turned toward Danny's face. Its markings had transformed into two narrow black eyes that now stared at him angrily. A sickening whisper came from its mouth, which was growing ever larger before Danny's eyes.

"Wha-a-a-a-a-a-a-a-a-a-a," it whispered as a line of smoke slid from its black mouth. Danny felt the smoke slowly wrap around his neck and pull him closer to the monstrous thing before him.

So frozen from fear, he didn't even notice the tugging at his feet until he was suddenly tumbling backward onto Desmond. They both landed on the ground with a thud. When Danny looked back at the fence, the monster was gone and the fence was back to normal.

"What was that?" Danny asked.

"That is your rescue plan flush-flush-flushing down the toy-toy-toilet."

Danny hated to admit it, but Desmond was right. There was no way Danny could get past that nasty fence. Poor Jingo! Stuck in that awful place all by himself.

"It's all my fault," Danny said sadly. He shivered in the cold and wrapped his arms around his body as he dropped to the ground. He'd really messed up. He lowered his head over his bent knees and fought back tears while Desmond muttered beside him.

"What a lot of noise you two are making," exclaimed a small voice.

Danny didn't look up. "Leave us alone in our misery!"

"Please excuse me, but what are you so upset about?" the voice asked kindly.

Danny choked back a sob, "My good friend is gone! Go-o-one forever!" Then he wagged his thumb at Desmond. "And that guy is just really, really hungry."

"You have a new friend?" the voice asked sadly, "Please, may I know who?"

That voice. Danny suddenly recognized it. Could it be? Was it possible? Danny looked up and saw a little blue boy with one leg, one arm, one ear, and no nose. A little bluer and tired than before, but there was no mistaking his friend.

"Jingo!" he cried. He jumped to his feet and threw his arms around him, clanking against his shoulders. "How did you get out? Those creatures are terrifying!"

Jingo pointed to the back of the building. "There's an exit on the other side. I opened the door and walked out."

"Oh," said Danny, looking at his feet. "But they think you're a virus! How did you escape?"

"They did tests and finally told me that I was right. I am not a virus. Then they said I was free to leave. So, I did."

"I'm sorry that I left you alone."

Jingo looked at Danny, "Why didn't you come back?"

"I did," Danny insisted, "I did. But you were gone!"

Jingo nodded. "Yes, a Disinfector spotted me and took me away."

"I'm so sorry. I didn't know. Are you okay?"

"I don't feel well. But I'm glad to be out of there."

"What happened to your nose?" asked Danny. "It's completely gone now."

Jingo raised his fingers to where his nose used

to be. "Oh no, I didn't know that. It must have happened in there." He pointed again at the building and as he did, the top half of his finger broke off and fell to the ground with a clank.

"Your finger!" Danny cried.

A frightened look crossed Jingo's face. "I'm losing my parts again. I must have been exposed to a real virus. I'm going to disappear just like my buddy Jango did when the virus hit."

"We can't let that happen. I won't let it!"

"I need to get back to the other side of the wall where I'm safe."

"Then we need to hurry." Danny turned to Desmond. "How do we get out of here?"

"You really wanta-wanta-wanta leave already-eddy-eddy?" he asked.

"Of course! Jingo is sick."

"But D-d-d-dan-o," he plastered a fake smile on his face, showing a set of yellow teeth that Danny hadn't noticed before. "More-mo-mo-more fun-fun. Let's have more fun!"

"I'm going home. If you don't want to help us, then we're leaving without you."

"No! I mean... let me eat-eat-eat you. I mean help-help you. Eat-eat later."

Danny looked hard at Desmond. He'd changed a lot since when they first met at the wall. Now he was taller, uglier, meaner, and boy, he smelled worse than his dad's running shoes. He wanted to leave him behind, but without his help would they find their way back to the wall? They could wander forever and never get out.

He looked at Jingo for advice, but his head was bent low and his body drooped like a marionette. Danny sighed. More choices. Following Desmond was the quickest way out of this mess, he decided.

"Oh, all right."

Jingo, too tired to hop along, wrapped his arms around one of Danny's legs and stepped onto his foot. He was so light that Danny barely felt his weight as he walked. Desmond skipped ahead of them. For an instant, Danny thought he saw a tail slip below his shorts. But it was gone before he got a second look.

Up, Down, In and Out

"I know-know-know a little shortcut-cut-cut," Desmond said with a smile that sent shivers down Danny's back.

They stopped in front of a small red swinging door. Desmond pushed it open and disappeared through it. Danny lifted Jingo onto his back.

"Can you hang onto my neck?" he asked. "I think we may need to move fast once we get in there."

Jingo nodded and held on. Clank! Another finger dropped to the ground.

"I'm disappearing," whispered Jingo.

"It'll be okay. I'll get you back." Danny created this mess, now he had to clean it up. Somehow, he had to get Jingo back to safety.

They went through the door and entered a long,

dark hallway. Desmond was nowhere to be seen but up ahead was a ladder suspended in air. Danny took a step toward it. Cr-r-rack!

"Ice," said Jingo.

Danny looked down. Cracks spread out under his foot. He took another step. Cr-r-r-rack! Black liquid slithered like worms through the broken ice. They had to move fast. Danny ran and slipped, but caught himself before falling down. With every step, his foot shattered the ground like a rock to a window.

"You can do it. Hurry!" whispered Jingo into his ear.

Behind him, whole chunks of floor dissolved into the black water. They were almost at the ladder now but the bottom rung was too high to reach.

"Hang on!"

Danny jumped and grabbed the lowest rung. They climbed halfway up before stopping to look below. The floor was gone. Only a sea of black swished beneath them.

"That was close," said Danny, shuddering. He climbed up the ladder and onto the next landing where they faced five corridors.

"Where do we go?" asked Danny.

"We're in some sort of maze. I don't know what way to go. Isn't Desmond supposed to lead us?" Jingo asked.

"That was the plan," agreed Danny. "Desmond!"

There was no answer.

"I don't know which way to go!" he cried.

"Each hallway looks exactly the same, so just pick one and see where it leads us."

"You're right. I just need to pick one."

Danny closed his eyes and spun around. When he stopped and opened his eyes he faced one of the hallways. That's the one they followed.

He raced through the corridor. It curved so that he could never see more than a few feet in front of him. When he finally reached the end, it led nowhere. A dead end.

"Oh great! I picked the wrong one."

He returned to the other openings and chose another route. At the end of it were three doors. One to their right, one to their left, and one in front.

He opened the one in front first. It led to another door. He opened that. Then there was another door, and another, and another, and another, and another.

"Aaaargh!" yelled Danny.

"Give up. These doors will not lead anywhere no matter how many we open," said Jingo.

Danny agreed. He ran back and opened the door on his left. There was nothing there. No walls. No floor. No light. Danny leaned his head in and peered inside. The darkness wrapped his cold body like a warm blanket on a wintry night. He pressed further into the dark and felt his body lift. Closing his eyes, he floated in, feeling light as a breeze. He was so sleepy.

"Danny," cried Jingo, "I can't hold on much longer!"

Danny's eyes flipped open. His body had been sucked into the dark. The only thing stopping him from being swallowed up forever was Jingo. His blue friend gripped the door knob while his leg clung to Danny's neck. Danny reached for the knob and pulled them both back into the hallway and slammed the door shut.

"I'm so sorry Jingo. If it weren't for you, we'd have been lost forever! It was so warm. I didn't want to leave."

"You were drifting away. Keep your eyes open, please!" Jingo said.

Danny grabbed the knob on the remaining door. It

opened to a white passageway. Finally! Danny ran as Jingo hung on. His legs hurt but he wouldn't stop until he reached the end. Keep going, keep going, he told himself as he fought the urge to slow down. Eventually, he ran out of breath and had to stop. Still there was no end in sight. The white hall went on and on.

"My legs are tired. Maybe we should turn around."

Jingo let go of Danny's neck and hopped beside him. "Is that better?" Jingo asked.

Danny felt bad about complaining. Having two aching legs was still better than having just one leg and one arm, like Jingo.

"I'm okay. I like carrying you."

Jingo looked up at him. "Thanks. But I'll hop for a bit."

"Do you think we'll ever get to the end?"

"Well, I think that if we stop, we'll get nowhere. So, please don't go back. There's nothing there."

"But we've been walking for so long!" Danny turned around and gasped.

"What?" Jingo asked.

"The door! It's right behind us!" Danny cried. "We haven't gone anywhere!"

"How is that possible?"

Danny picked up Jingo and ran, trying to get as far from the door as possible. It worked. The door was further behind them now, so at least he knew they were actually getting somewhere. But when he stopped to catch his breath, he sensed some movement. The door was right behind them again. They had to keep moving, otherwise the door would push them to the end of the hallway. And what was at the end? Danny could only hope that it wasn't a wall.

They turned a corner and were relieved to discover that the end of the corridor opened up into a grey room. Anything was better than a wall. Once they reached the opening, they realized that the space wasn't a room, after all. It was just billows of smoke swirling up into the air, and the floor just dropped like a cliff into it. The door careened toward them like a freight train now. They had to jump.

"Hold on, little buddy!" Danny yelled.

Desmond on the Loose

Danny bent his knees and bounded off the cliff into the smoke. But instead of falling through the clouds of smoke, he landed on top of them. The smoky shapes tossed him and Jingo around like wrestlers. One second he was on his back, the next on his bum, the next on his head. Jingo held onto Danny as tight as he could.

They were at the mercy of these strange mists until Danny realized that the shapes weren't trying to hurt them. In fact, they flowed just like ocean waves, sweeping over him one after the other. Once he figured that out, he was able to figure out when the next wave would crash. Instead of falling under, as he had been doing, he jumped on top of the smoke and surfed it until they reached another ledge.

"Oh, D-d-d-a-a-a-nny!" echoed a voice from below.

"Huh?" Danny looked down.

"What is that?" asked Jingo nervously.

Perched on an elevator lift moving up toward them was a creature that raced chills up Danny's spine. Its face was lumpy as cookie dough and black bits floated around its head like fruit flies over a rotting peach. It had a crooked mouth with no lips and a long tongue dangled out of it, dripping with drool. Its toad-like legs bounced up and down like a spring, and a scaly tail spiked behind it.

The monster was dressed in the same t-shirt and blue jeans that Desmond had been wearing. But it couldn't be, thought Danny, it couldn't possibly be him.

"Run!" yelled Jingo.

Danny turned to run.

"Don-don't do it!" croaked the creature.

The voice! It was the same voice Danny heard just before seeing the button on the computer screen. It was him!

"Why so fraidy-fraidy-fraidy?" the creature asked, "It's me-me-me."

A hammering laugh shook the maze.

Danny stopped and stammered, "Desmond? What happened? You're not a boy! You're disgusting!"

"Gee, thanka-thanka-thanks," he answered, "You know-know-know, you're notta-notta-notta perfect. Like how you-you-you snort after you talka-talka-talk?"

"No I don't!" Danny said with a snort.

"All righty-tighty-tighty. Let's not fighta-fighta-fighta," Desmond said.

"What happened to you?" Danny asked.

"That fuddy-duddy-fuddy kiddy with the orange hair-hair?" Desmond laughed, "You are a silly-frilly-silly boy! I fool-fool-fooled you! I am whata-whata-what I want you to think I am. How else would I get you to koo-koo-come with me? Not-tot-tot if I looked like this. But if I look-look like a kid... Easy-peasy-peasy."

The elevator rose nearer to Danny and Jingo. Soon, he'd be close enough to jump.

"So, you just want to play with me?" Danny asked, trying not to look at his face.

"No," Desmond answered calmly, "Play time is over. I'm hung-dung-hungry. Now I ca-ca-catch you, then roast-toast-toast you, and eat-eat-eat you!

Maybe save-save baked toe-toe-toes for a late snack-ack-ack."

"No!" Danny screamed.

"Okay-kay-kay. I'll eat-eat you all at once! And destroy that little boo-boo-blue friend of yours for once and for all-all-all."

"Run!" yelled Jingo.

This time, Danny listened.

Always a Way Out

Danny sprinted across the floor where he came across…

"Another door!" cried Danny and Jingo together.

They didn't have time to consider what horrors lay behind it. A sickening slap of toad feet landed close by. Danny swung the door open and entered a damp, dark cave. The only source of light came from Danny and Jingo. They glowed like flashlights. He followed a twisted path through the tunnel, turning one way then another. Danny had no idea where he was going. He could only hope that Desmond was just as confused as he. A staircase emerged. He bounded up the steps two at a time.

"Stinky-stinky-stinky feet yummy-tummy-tummy treat that I want to eat-eat-eat," Desmond's muttering voice droned on as his legs flip flopped toward them.

When Danny reached the top of the stairs something scratched his face. He crouched down and reached into the dark air. What was that? he wondered.

"Bats!" whispered Jingo.

Once his eyes got used to the darkness, he could see what Jingo meant. The ceiling was alive with silvery bats crisscrossing the air like a checker board. When he tried standing again, another bat clawed at his hair. He dropped back to the ground and crawled.

Desmond chanted miserably, "Danny-Danny-Danny boy. My favourite-favourite toy-toy-toy. I'll eat the crusty-crusty-scabbies, boil them off your knobbly-knees."

Danny shuddered.

"Don't listen to him," warned Jingo. "Keep going."

"Did you know that he was really a monster?" Danny whispered back.

"No. But I've heard of them. Desmond's a hoobogey. He's not the only one around here. There are lots of them. They can look like boys and girls right after they've eaten. That's when they trick kids like you into playing with them so they can drag you into their world. But when they're hungry again, they morph back to their real selves. That's when their new little friend turns into dinner. Desmond won't stop until he's caught you."

"Not if I can stop him first," Danny said bravely.

"How are you going to do that?"

Danny frowned. "I haven't figured that part out yet."

The bat cave ended and they climbed along the edge of a mountain that was made up of stones that looked like bowling balls. Danny wobbled across them, using his hands to keep him steady. His foot became lodged between two stones. He tried to pull it out, but the rocks would not budge.

Close by, Desmond sang, "Chompa-chompa-chompa on a Danny rumpa-rumpa."

"Hurry!" Jingo cried. "Or is this part of your plan?"

"No! No plan! I'm stuck." He kicked the stones with his free foot as hard as he could.

"Ow!" Danny rubbed his throbbing big toe. Gripping the stone over his foot with both hands, he heaved with all his might. Jingo jumped off Danny's back and tugged at it, too. Thoughts about home floated through Danny's mind. He thought about his brother. He thought about his mom and dad. And strangely, he didn't think at all about his computer.

Just when he was about to give up hope, the stone loosened and fell over the side of the mountain.

"Finally!" Danny yelled, "Let's go!"

He lifted his free foot. Jingo climbed up onto Danny's back and they continued along the side of the mountain. The stone rumbled down, down, down the long slope… kickakakaka-kickakakaka.

"That's been falling a long time," Jingo said.

Danny stopped for an instant and listened. It didn't sound like just one stone tripping down the hill. He peered over his shoulder.

"Hold on!" he yelled, "The mountain is collapsing!"

Stones spilled like marbles under their feet as the mountain broke apart. He scrambled across the rolling rocks and reached level ground as the avalanche crashed below. Danny raced through the black tunnel, keeping his eyes on his feet to make sure he didn't trip or get them caught in anything else. Then BAM! He smacked into a wall and dropped like a swatted fly.

"My head," groaned Danny, his eyes shut, "Oooh, my head. And another… dead end… We're stuck… No going back."

A hand touched his shoulder. Danny opened his eyes to see Jingo's face over his.

"There's always a way out." Jingo pointed up.

There, in the ceiling just above him, was an opening. Danny rose to his feet, rubbing his head. He lifted first Jingo, then himself, through the hole to the next level. Another opening was above that one. They climbed through that one, and kept climbing one floor to the next until reaching the very top.

They could have been on top of a sky scraper. There was no ceiling nor any walls and ten steps in any direction would send them over the edge into a black abyss. They had nowhere else to go. They were trapped. Danny reached into his pocket and found a pack of gum under all the coins he'd collected earlier. He opened it and started stuffing the pieces in his mouth.

"Want one?" he asked with a full mouth before finishing the pack.

Jingo shook his head.

"You know," Jingo said, "You're the best friend I've ever had."

"Me... too," Danny agreed between chews. "I... have a... plan."

Jingo nodded. "Your timing is perfect."

"Have some gum," Danny said. "I insist."

A Sticky Situation

When Desmond lifted his lumpy head through the opening, he saw Jingo. Desmond half-croaked, half-growled at the sight of him.

"You! You're not-tot-tot worth my-my-my time," Desmond spat out as he slapped his wide feet onto the floor. "Where's the tasty-tasty-tasty toy-toy-boy?"

Jingo pointed a finger. "Behind you."

Desmond turned around.

"It's payback time!" Danny cried. He pulled his hands from his pockets and threw all his coins into Desmond's face.

Startled, Desmond covered his head and stepped backward, giving Danny just enough time to ram into him. He forced that slimy body to the edge where Jingo had laid himself down. Desmond tripped on Jingo and tumbled over the cliff.

"No-no-no-o-o-o-o!" he yelled, grabbing Jingo in a last ditch effort to save himself and pulled him down with him. Danny watched in horror as Jingo disappeared.

"Jingo-o-o-o-o-o!" Danny screamed.

They were both gone. Danny ran to the edge and looked down.

"Why, hello!" said Jingo, who hung by his blue shirt as if it was attached to a hook. "Can you give me a hand?" he asked.

"It worked!" Danny said, relieved. He pulled his friend up to safety.

"Thanks for the bubble gum. I did need it after all," Jingo said. He unstuck a wad of gum from the front of his shirt.

Danny rolled the gum into a ball and put it in his pocket. "I'm keeping this one for good luck! And I don't want to waste it. It still has lots of flavour. Now how do we get out of here and back to the wall?"

The sound of flapping wings made them both look up. A familiar boy with wheels for feet was flying over them. It was the gooligan who had helped lead Danny to Jingo. Danny waved. He waved back and dropped a blue ball. It bounced at their feet then

dropped off the side, forming a slide that curved into the darkness.

"He's showing us the way out!" cried Danny. He lifted Jingo onto his lap and jumped onto the slide. They flew along the blue path through the dark and into light where Danny could see the massive wall where he met Desmond getting closer and closer. The slide curved past the wagons and the rides, video screens, and huge scrolls of paper. Soon they'd be back in Blah Land. And Danny couldn't wait. Next thing he knew, they had slid through a hole in the wall that was just the right fit for Danny and Jingo.

"We made it," said Jingo with relief. For once, Danny was thrilled to be surrounded by his boring old games. Here he was safe.

"Will you be okay now?" Danny asked, looking at Jingo's hand with the missing fingers.

"Yes," said Jingo. "I'll miss you, Danny. You're the first friend I've had since Jango."

"I'll miss you too, Jingo." Danny hugged him. Jingo was cold as ice. "Brrrrr, you're freezing!" Danny shivered.

"No, I'm fine. It's you that's freezing. All kids get that way after being in here too long."

"But I didn't notice how cold it was before."

"You will freeze if you stay in this world for too long."

"But you never get cold?"

"No. I don't know what it's like to be warm. It must feel very nice," said Jingo. "But I won't freeze without it."

Danny thought about the warm fire in his family room, his warm bed at night, his parents' warm hugs. Suddenly he missed his home terribly.

"Danny... Danny," his mother's voice floated out to them.

"That's my mom!" Danny shouted. "I've got to go."

"Danny Lenesky. Stop ignoring me. I'm talking to you," she continued.

Jingo pulled something out from his pocket and handed it to Danny.

"Here. Take this," Jingo said, "So that you never forget me." He handed Danny what appeared to be a long blue stone. Danny rubbed it in his hand.

"It's your finger!" he said, "Don't you need this?"

"No. I can't attach it again. But I can still feel with it. When you hold it, I'll know you're thinking of me."

"Thanks. I'll always remember you," Danny

hugged him one last time and pushed the glass finger into his pant pocket. "I gotta go."

Jingo pointed toward the sound of Danny's mom. "Just follow your mom's voice. You'll find your way back."

"Danny! Turn off the computer," his mother said from a distance.

Within seconds Danny was flying through the twisting tunnel and before he could say 'Jingo Jango' he was back in his chair.

"Mom!" he cried out.

His mother's hands were set firmly on her hips and her eyebrows were wrinkled.

"Well, welcome back. I've only said your name about ten times," she said. "It's like you're in another world when you're on that computer."

"Well...," Danny answered.

"Never mind. Just turn it off and set the table for dinner." She rested a hand on his shoulder and his entire body tingled with warmth.

"Sure," answered Danny, grateful for the first time in his life to hear the *Mom Bomb*. When she left the room, he pulled Jingo's finger out and looked at it. Back in the real world it looked like a really neat stone. Long and blue, shiny as a mirror and smooth as a kitten's tail.

"Jingo," Danny whispered. The stone flashed.

"I won't forget you," he said, and returned it to his pocket.

Danny clicked on 'Shut Down' and got up to leave. He'd miss Jingo, but it was nice to be home, too. Back where he belonged. Now all he had to do was figure out how to get out of setting the table.

THE END.

RECYCLED
Paper made from
recycled material
FSC® C021757

MARQUIS
Marquis Book Printing Inc.

Québec, Canada
2011

Printed on Silva Enviro 100% post-consumer EcoLogo certified paper,
processed chlorine free and manufactured using biogas energy.